ISBN 1 85854 515 3
Published by Brimax Books Ltd, Newmarket, England, CB8 7AU 1996.
Printed in Dubai.

My Easy to Read
FAIRYTALES

Illustrated by
Gill Guile

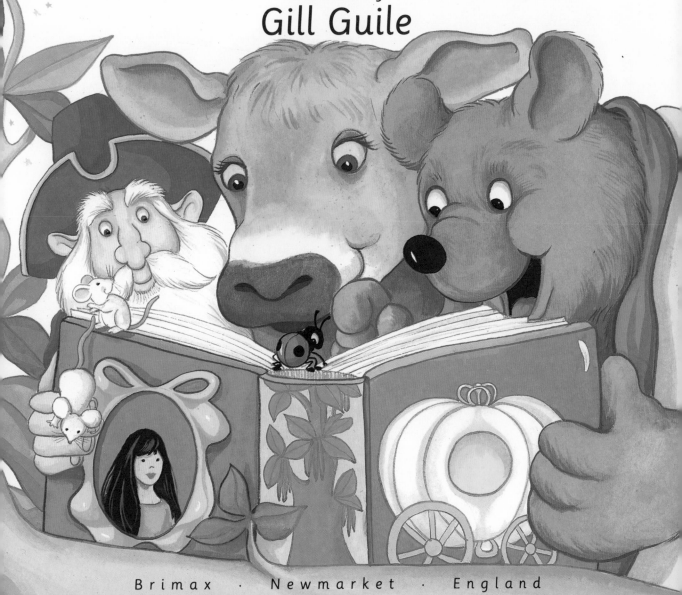

Brimax · Newmarket · England

Cinderella

Cinderella lives in a big house with her two ugly sisters.
Her sisters are unkind to her and make her do all the housework.
They make her dust and polish, wash the clothes, do the dishes, and help them get ready when they want to go out.

One day a letter arrives for the ugly sisters. It is an invitation to a ball at the palace!

"Am I invited?" asks Cinderella.

"Of course not!" says one of the sisters. "You have to help us get ready. You can't go!"

"Besides," says the other sister, "You don't have a dress. You only have those rags!"

On the day of the ball, Cinderella helps her sisters get ready. She washes their dresses and polishes their shoes. By the time they have gone, Cinderella is so tired she sits by the fire and sobs. "I wish I could go to the ball!" she cries.

Suddenly she hears a voice. "Don't worry. You shall go to the ball!"

"Who are you?" asks Cinderella. She is frightened.

"I am your fairy godmother," says the stranger. "I will get you ready for the ball."

"Bring me a big pumpkin!" says the fairy godmother. She touches it with her wand and turns it into a coach. Next, Cinderella brings her four white mice. The fairy godmother turns them into white horses. She turns three lizards into a coach driver and two footmen. She turns Cinderella's rags into a gown. On Cinderella's feet are a pair of glass slippers.

"Now you are ready to go," says the fairy godmother. "But remember to leave before the clock strikes midnight. At twelve o'clock your dress will turn to rags and your coach will turn back into a pumpkin!" Cinderella sets off in the coach to the ball.

When Cinderella arrives at the ball she sees her two sisters. They do not know who she is. Cinderella dances with the Prince all night long. He will not dance with anyone else. Cinderella is very happy. She forgets her fairy godmother's warning about leaving before midnight.

Suddenly the clock strikes twelve! Cinderella runs out of the palace and down the steps. Her dress turns into rags and the coach becomes a pumpkin again. As she runs away, one of her glass slippers falls off. The Prince finds it. He says to a footman, "Find the girl who owns this slipper. I want to marry her."

The footman searches the land for the owner of the slipper. Finally he comes to Cinderella's house. Her sisters try on the glass slipper. It does not fit either of them. Cinderella tries it on. The slipper fits perfectly. The Prince marries Cinderella and they live happily ever after.

Can you find five differences between these two pictures?

Can you say these words and tell the story by yourself?

glass slipper

Cinderella

pumpkin

wand

27

Goldilocks and the Three Bears

The three bears live in a small cottage in the forest. Every morning they have porridge for breakfast. One morning the porridge is too hot. The bears decide to go for a walk while the porridge cools.

Goldilocks is walking in the forest, too. She sees the three bears' cottage. She opens the door and goes inside. Goldilocks sees the bowls of porridge. She tastes some from the big bowl, some from the middle-sized bowl and some from the little bowl. The porridge in the little bowl tastes best of all. Goldilocks eats it all up.

33

Goldilocks sees three chairs.
She sits in the biggest chair.
It is too hard. She sits in the
middle-sized chair. It is too
soft. She sits in the little
chair. It is just right.
But Goldilocks is too heavy.
The little chair breaks.

35

Goldilocks goes upstairs. She sees three beds. Goldilocks lies on the big bed. It is too hard. She lies on the middle-sized bed. It is too soft. She lies on the little bed. It is just right. Goldilocks falls fast asleep.

When the three bears arrive home, Father Bear says in his loud voice, "Someone has been eating my porridge."
Mother Bear says in her soft voice, "Someone has been eating my porridge."
Then Baby Bear says in his tiny voice, "Someone has been eating my porridge, too. Look! It is all gone!"

Father Bear sits down in his chair to think. "Someone has been sitting in my chair," he says in his loud voice. "Someone has been sitting in my chair," Mother Bear says in her soft voice. "Someone has been sitting in my chair," Baby Bear says in his tiny voice. "Look! It is broken!"

Baby Bear starts to cry.
The three bears decide to look
upstairs. "Someone has been
lying on my bed," Father Bear
says in his loud voice.
"Someone has been lying on my
bed," Mother Bear says in her
soft voice.
"Someone has been lying on my
bed," Baby Bear says in his
tiny voice. "And there she is!"

Goldilocks wakes up and sees the three bears standing in front of her. They look very angry. Goldilocks jumps up, runs downstairs and out of the cottage. She does not stop until she reaches home.

Now the three bears always make sure that the cottage door is locked when they go for a walk in the forest. They do not want anyone else eating their porridge, breaking their chairs or sleeping in their beds.

Can you find five differences between these two pictures?

Can you say these words and tell the story by yourself?

chair

porridge

Baby Bear

Goldilocks

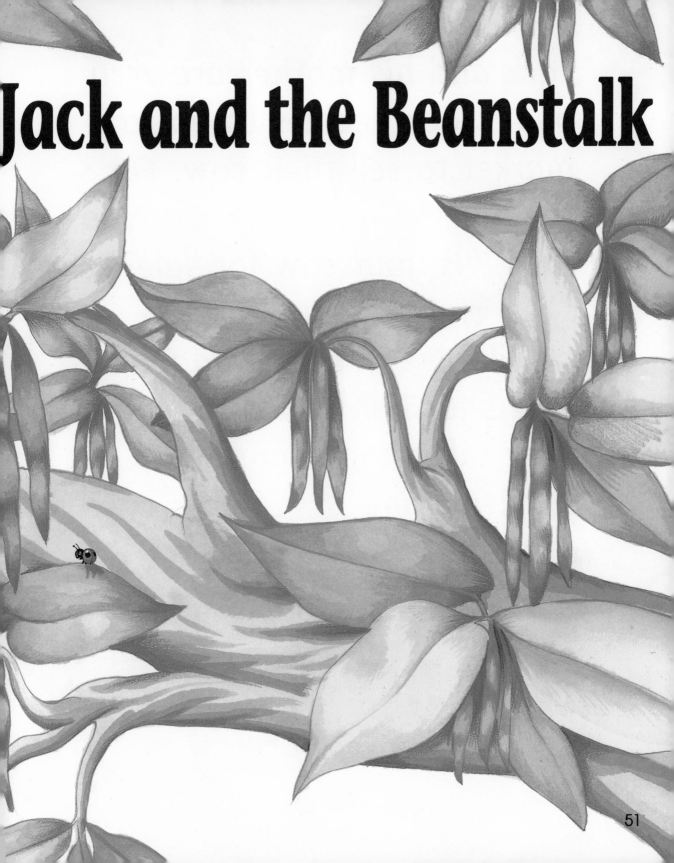

Jack and the Beanstalk

Jack and his mother are very poor. Jack decides to go to market to sell their cow. On the way he meets a man who says, "Is your cow for sale?" "Yes, she is," says Jack.
"I will give you five magic beans for her," says the man. Jack takes the beans and hurries home.

Jack's mother is very angry when she hears what Jack has done. She throws the beans out of the window and sends Jack to bed without any supper. When Jack wakes up the next day, there is an enormous beanstalk outside his bedroom window.

Jack decides to climb up the beanstalk. He climbs higher and higher until he finds himself in another world above the clouds. He walks along a path until he comes to a huge house. He knocks as hard as he can on the door. It is opened by a giant's wife. She invites Jack in and gives him some breakfast.

While Jack is still eating he hears heavy footsteps and a loud voice shouting, "Fee-fi-fo-fum, I smell the blood of an Englishman!"

"That is my husband," says the woman. "You must hide in the oven. He likes to eat boys like you for breakfast."

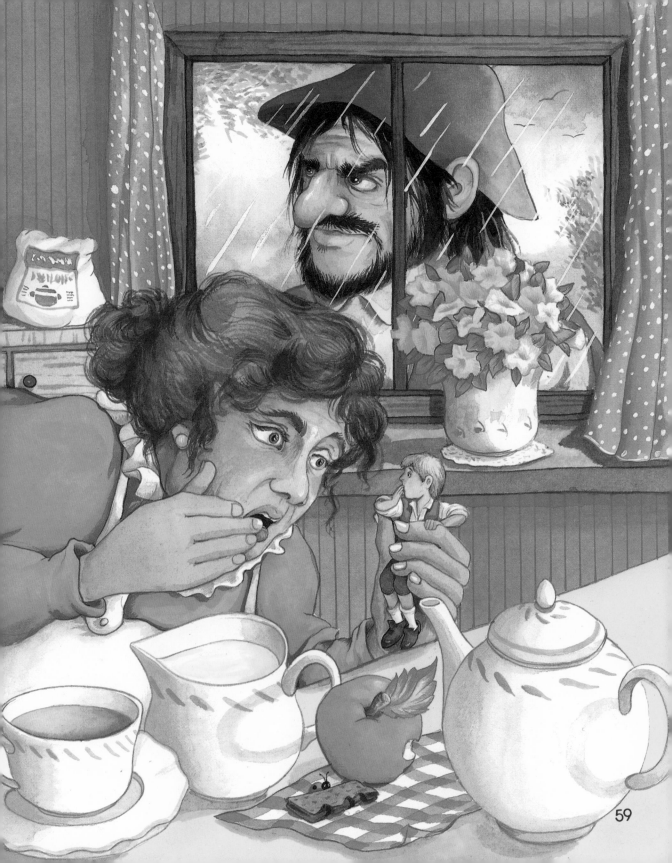

The giant is sure he can smell a boy, but he cannot find Jack. After his breakfast, the giant asks for his magic hen. Jack peeks out of the oven. The giant says, "Lay, hen!" and the hen lays a golden egg.

"Mother would like to own a hen like that," whispers Jack.

Jack waits until the giant is asleep. He picks up the hen and tucks it inside his shirt. He sneaks from the house, runs along the path and climbs down the beanstalk. He gives the magic hen to his mother. She is very pleased to see Jack.

The next morning, Jack climbs up the beanstalk again. He slips under the giant's door and hides in the kitchen drawer. "Fee-fi-fo-fum, I smell the blood of an Englishman!" roars the giant. He looks for Jack but cannot find him. Then the giant calls for his golden harp and says, "Play, harp!" The harp plays without the giant touching the strings.

When the giant falls asleep, Jack creeps out of the drawer. As he picks up the harp it calls, "Master! Wake up!" The giant roars with anger at Jack. He chases him out of the house and along the path until they reach the beanstalk. Jack climbs down as fast as he can. His mother hands him an axe. With one mighty blow, Jack cuts through the beanstalk.

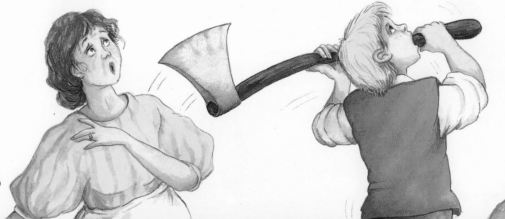

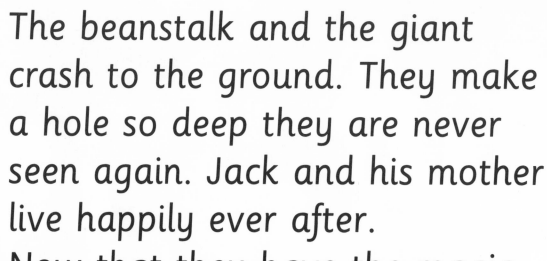

The beanstalk and the giant crash to the ground. They make a hole so deep they are never seen again. Jack and his mother live happily ever after.

Now that they have the magic hen that lays golden eggs and the harp that sings by itself, they will never be poor again.

69

Can you find five differences between these two pictures?

Can you say these words and find the things in the picture?

magic hen

giant

harp

beanstalk

Snow White
and the Seven Dwarfs

Snow White lives in a big castle with her step-mother the Queen. Every day the Queen says to her magic mirror, "Mirror, mirror on the wall, who is the fairest of them all?" Every day the mirror says, "You, oh Queen, are the fairest in the land."

One day the Queen says to her mirror, "Mirror, mirror on the wall, who is the fairest of them all?" The mirror says, "You, oh Queen, are very fair; but Snow White is the fairest in the land." The Queen sees Snow White's face in the mirror. She is very angry.

The Queen tells her huntsman to take Snow White into the forest and kill her. But the huntsman lets Snow White go. She wanders through the forest until she sees a cottage. No one is at home so Snow White opens the door and goes in.

79

What a messy cottage it is!
Snow White decides to clean up.
She washes seven plates, seven
cups, seven knives, seven forks
and seven spoons. She dusts
seven little chairs and makes
seven little beds. Soon she is
so tired she falls fast asleep.
Seven dwarfs live in the cottage.
When they arrive home, they are
surprised to find Snow White.
They decide to let her stay.

One day, the Queen says to her magic mirror, "Mirror, mirror on the wall, who is the fairest of them all?" The mirror says, "You, oh Queen, are very fair; but Snow White, who lives in the forest with the little men, is the fairest in the land." The Queen is very angry. She decides to find Snow White.

The Queen dresses up as an old woman. She fills a basket with apples and goes to look for Snow White. The dwarfs are working in the forest. When the Queen finds their cottage she knocks on the door. "Will you buy an apple?" she asks Snow White. But this is a special apple.
The Queen has put a spell on it. Snow White takes one bite and falls to the floor as if dead.

When the dwarfs arrive home, they find Snow White lying on the floor. "The wicked Queen has been here," they say sadly. The dwarfs think Snow White is dead. They make a special bed for her in the forest. All the birds and animals keep watch around her.

One day, a Prince rides through the forest. He sees Snow White lying on her bed. He says to the dwarfs, "Please let me take her home with me." As the Prince lifts Snow White up, the piece of magic apple falls from her mouth. Snow White opens her eyes. She is alive!

That day, the Queen asks her magic mirror, "Mirror, mirror on the wall, who is the fairest of them all?" The mirror says, "You, oh Queen, are very fair; but Snow White is the fairest in the land." The Queen is so angry she flies into a rage and dies. Snow White marries the Prince and they both live happily ever after.

Can you find five differences between these two pictures?

Can you say these words and find the things in the picture?

Snow White

Queen

cottage

apple